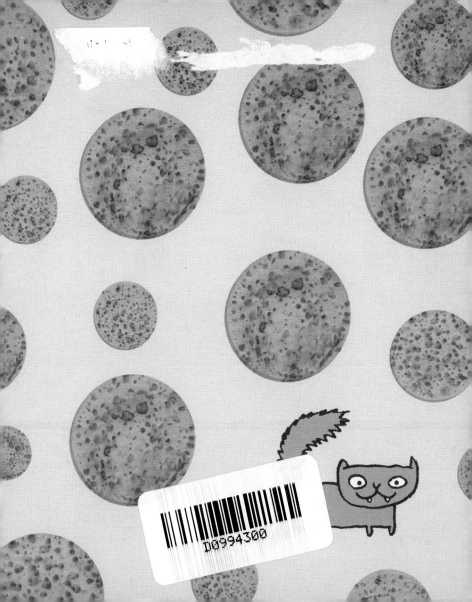

A Crumpety Calamity

PIP STREET

A Crumpety Calamity

Jo Simmons

Illustrated by Steve Wells

SCHOLASTIC

First published in the UK in 2013 by Scholastic Children's Books
An imprint of Scholastic Ltd
Euston House, 24 Eversholt Street
London, NW1 1DB, UK
Registered office: Westfield Road, Southam, Warwickshire, CV47 0RA
SCHOLASTIC and associated logos are trademarks and/
or registered trademarks of Scholastic Inc.

ISBN 978 1 407 13282 2

A CIP catalogue record for this book is available
from the British Library.

Printed and bound by CPI Group (UK) Ltd, Croydon, CR0 4YY
Papers used by Scholastic Children's Books are made from
wood grown in sustainable forests.

1 3 5 7 9 10 8 6 4 2

This is a work of fiction. Names, characters, places, incidents
and dialogues are products of the author's imagination or are used fictitiously.
Any resemblance to actual people, living or dead, events
or locales is entirely coincidental.

www.scholastic.co.uk/zone
www.visitpipstreet.com

For Eleanor, Joe, Olivia and Rosa,

for reading and reviewing those early drafts

1
Summertime and the Living is Crumpety

It was a beautiful summer's day on Pip Street, as quiet and peaceful as a tea bag. In the garden of number 4, Bobby Cobbler and his tiny best friend Imelda Small were lying on the grass. Imelda was wearing a deep-sea diver's costume, for no particular reason. Conkers, Bobby's cool and brilliant black cat, was snoozing in the flower bed, dreaming of wrestling a tiger. And a ladybird called Keith was eating a greenfly called... Oh dear, too late. We will never know his name...

Anyway, apart from Keith murdering greenflies, life had been lovely and peaceful since all that funny business with the Pip Street pussycats going missing.* The cats had been found and the culprit sent packing, and all thanks to Bobby

* The funny business of which I speak is all in A Whiskery Mystery. Haven't read it yet? Get down to your local bookshop smartish. No, wait! Finish this one first...

and Imelda's clever plans and daring doings. And so, with no mysteries to solve for now, the two children were staring up at the sky, enjoying some pondering time.

Imelda was humming her favourite song, "Have You Seen the Mushroom Man?" (which is a bit like that one about the muffin man, only more mushroomy) and thinking, *Do clouds have feelings?* as a cloud shaped like a massive cross hedgehog drifted by.

Bobby was thinking: *Who would win in a fight between a bear and a lion?* (I'll tell you – the bear, on account of its mighty paws. Shh! Our secret.)

"All this pondering is making me hungry," said Imelda, sitting up suddenly and yanking off her diver's mask and snorkel.

"Me, too," said Bobby, and they went into the kitchen to get some crumpets.

Why crumpets? Why not jam sandwiches? Or choccie biccies? Or plums? Because crumpets were all there was to eat in Bobby's house. There were sixty-five in the cupboard, forty-three in the freezer, ten in the bread bin, two in the oven and one on top of the clock.

Since Bobby's dad had become manager of the local crumpet factory, a blizzard of crumpets had blown through the house. Bobby had been eating them for every meal. He was growing tired of them. Crumpet fatigue had set in. He longed for a simple crusty roll; an unassuming cracker; a soft, floury bap.

But no.

It was

crumpets

crumpets

always crumpets.

With a sigh, Bobby popped two crumpets in the toaster and flicked through the local paper, *The Daily Wotsit*, while they crisped up.

The headlines were:

MAN ARRESTED FOR THROWING YOGHURT AT SEAGULLS

Local woman slightly hurt in accident with duvet

Overweight Labrador dog "as big as pregnant pony" says astounded vet

Hmm, mused Bobby, *there* are *a lot of fat Labradors around*. He could think of four living on neighbouring Dip Street and Chip Street alone.

Suddenly, *spring!* went the toaster and out flew the crumpets, like teatime treats wearing jet packs.

Imelda and Bobby were just tucking in when Bobby's dad came home from work, looking glum. Mr Cobbler often looked glum, but today he looked glummer. For he had bad news.

"Crumpet sales are down in the crumpet dumps," he said. "If I can't find a way to sell more, the factory will close, I'll be out of a job and we'll have to move again."

7

Bobby's crumpet fell from his hand, landing on his plate with a dull, doughy thud. Move again? *Again?* Bobby had moved eleven times in the nine years of his life. And besides, he loved living on Pip Street. It was better than all the other places his family had lived put together and multiplied by sixty-seven. Mainly because he had Imelda as his neighbour and tip-top friend.

"Oh Mr C, you absolutely one hundred per cent cannot move," blurted Imelda, wiping butter from her tiny chin. "You just got here. And besides, I like Bobby to bits – we are best mates!"

Everyone looked sad and lost and tearful. Even Conkers. Actually not Conkers, he mainly just looked black and fluffy. Plus he was still outside anyway. So, you know, whatever. . .

What could be done? Maybe crumpets had had their day. Maybe they were the penny-farthings of the snack world – outdated, awkward and a bit weird.

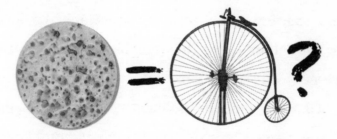

"We need to find a way to get everyone excited about crumpets again," said Bobby, and with this, he fired up his brain and got ready for a really good think.

2
Can Crumpets Be Cool?

Bobby thought and thought. Luckily, Bobby was good at thinking. It was one of his specialities, along with reading, making-of-plans and having

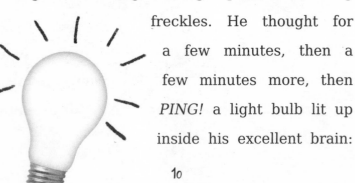

freckles. He thought for a few minutes, then a few minutes more, then *PING!* a light bulb lit up inside his excellent brain:

a light bulb glowing with crumpety inspiration.

"What about a competition?" he said. "To develop a new, amazing, taste-tastic crumpet?"

"Go on," said his dad, looking intrigued.

"Well, it's true, crumpets can be a bit boring," said Bobby. "Why are they always plain? Why can't they be stuffed or dipped or iced or *something*?

Well maybe they can! Let's launch a competition to see who can come up with the tastiest new crumpet. The prize would be having the crumpets named after you and sold throughout the land."

"I like it," said Bobby's dad, his eyes sparkling with hope and excitement (and hay fever). "If we can make people passionate about crumpets again, sales will pick up and we won't need to move."

"Exactly," said Bobby, wiping his fingers on his trousers – the favourite wiping location of all young boys – before jumping up. "Come on, Imelda. There must be a way to put the *mmmm* back into crummmmpets!"

3
New Arrivals on Pip Street

Meanwhile, back in the garden, Conkers stretched and sat up. He was just licking his chest, his eyes shut and his head full of how smart he was going to look any minute now, when a shrill *beep beep beep* smashed into his ears.

Conkers' eyes pinged open. His tongue froze mid-lick, poking out from his mouth a bit.

This was the only time Conkers looked less than very cool indeed. Quickly, he put his tongue in, but his little kitty mind was racing. What was that beeping? Was it a massive high-speed super-charged robot dog programmed to destroy all cats? He tiptoed along the garden wall and looked across the road. Oh, it wasn't a massive

high-speed super-charged robot dog. Phew. It was a removal van. A big one. It had backed into a space outside number 3 and now two men were carrying furniture in.

There was a boy outside, too, carrying bags into the house.

THIS IS A REMOVAL VAN

He was handsome, with a face like a pop star – a really good-looking one with excellent hair. Or that's what Conkers would have thought, if he had known about pop stars. But he didn't. He was just a cat, after all.

Conkers growled. Yes, cats do growl. No, really, they do. Look, I don't have time to argue. Why was Conkers growling? That's what matters here. Why the feline fretting? Why the cat consternation? What's up, pussycat?

"I don't have a good feeling about this new neighbour," Conkers would be saying, if he could speak. But we all know cats can't speak English. Even the English ones.

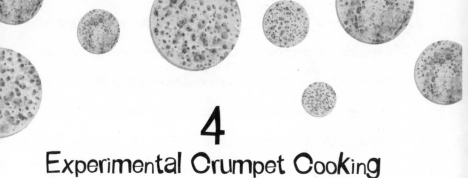

4
Experimental Crumpet Cooking

While Conkers watched the removal lorry being unloaded, Bobby and Imelda were in Bobby's kitchen, experimenting with different crumpet fillings.

They were like mad scientists who love toasted snacks more than secret formulas for world domination. They had stuffed crumpets with jam, cream cheese, chocolate, tomato soup. Imelda had even stuffed one with cheese and onion crisps. It wasn't nice.

"I think we're getting somewhere," said Bobby.

"I think we're getting in a mess," said Imelda, picking some cream cheese out of her ear.

18

"Crumpet making doesn't get tougher than this," said Bobby.

He stared at their creations.

"I like the stickiness of the jam, and the meltingness of the chocolate," he said. "I think we need a mix of sticky and sweet."

Bobby thought for a while, then rushed up to his room.

Imelda was left alone, with only a large blob of jam up her nose for company. She was just working it loose when Bobby sprinted back into the kitchen holding a box.

"Look!" he cried.

"A box!" said Imelda. "I like it. *Boxy!*"

"Not just any box," said Bobby. "These are

Scottish toffees from my Great Auntie Mo, who lives in faraway Glen Haggis," he explained. "We can mix them with some special ingredients to create our filling. But first, we need to melt them down."

"Here, let me do that," said Bobby's dad, returning to the kitchen as Bobby was tipping the toffees into a saucepan.

As the toffees slowly melted, Mr Cobbler told

the children about the new neighbours he had just met.

"Paddy and Patricia Pasty," he said. "They have a son called Pompey, too. Smashing boy, very charming, ten years old. I suggested he drop round sometime to play with you two."

Bobby and Imelda looked at each other. A new child on the street. Was this good or bad? Was there room in their hearts for another friend? Room in their lives? Room in the spaceship they had made from a cardboard box? (It was already a bit snug for two, to be honest.)

Enough questions, said Bobby, in his brain, noticing that the toffees were ready. It was time to get to work.

I cannot reveal the secret ingredients Bobby and Imelda added to Great Auntie Mo's toffees, because then they wouldn't be secret, would they? Let's just say it was some yummy stuff, some flavoursome sprinkles and plenty of tasty smatterings, too.

Bobby carefully spooned the brown gloop into the centre of a crumpet while Imelda looked on. Then they bit into it.

Ahhh... And also, *oooohhhh...* And definitely *mmmmmm...* It was as if their mouths had won the lottery and magic fireworks were going off in their brains, scattering sparkles of pure loveliness. They had done it. Success! Eureka! Joy to the world! The crumpet was crispy on the outside, soft on the inside, and a river of sweet toffee flowed into the children's mouths as they chewed.

They looked at each other, licking their toffee chops.

"*Gooooood*," said Bobby, but only once he had finished chewing. It's not nice to talk with your mouth full, after all.

"We could call it the Bobelda Bizzer," said Imelda. "Or the Bobtastic Imelda-Crum! Or, or, or. . ."

"Or what about the Sweet Feast!" said Bobby.

"Or the Can't-Be-Beaten, Only-Eaten Crumpet," suggested Imelda.

"The Unbeatable Eatable Crumpet," laughed Bobby.

The two children collapsed into giggles. Finally, Bobby calmed down.

"Let's just call it The King Crumpet," he said.

"Nice!" said Imelda, clapping her hands together. "The King will win and everyone will go bonkers for these and buy millions of packets and then you get to stay on Pip Street! Long live The King!"

"Remember, though," said Bobby. "Don't tell *anyone* the recipe. It must remain strictly at MCS level."

"MCS?" said Imelda.

"Maximum Crumpet Security," said Bobby. "If anyone finds out what we've created, if they realize just how delicious it is, they might want to steal the idea. It's unlikely, I know. I reckon everyone's going to get as excited about new crumpets as we are. But better safe than sorry, especially when The King is involved!"

5
Enter the Pasty

While Bobby and Imelda were creating their new crumpet, Mr Cobbler organized the competition. The final tasting would take place at the crumpet factory in one week's time, and top TV chef Drew Furry Windowsill would be the judge. Then, to spread the word, Mr Cobbler took out an advert in *The Daily Wotsit* and had colourful flyers made, which he posted through doors and left on shop counters.

27

Almost immediately, crumpet fever swept through the neighbourhood as people started experimenting with fillings and toppings. The Co-op sold out of crumpets and other tasty ingredients, such as chocolate, syrup and salami. Nathan, Imelda's hugely tall brother, became obsessed with creating a multicoloured crumpet, while Mrs Rhubarb, who lived next door to Bobby and was an actor, was spending hours in her kitchen perfecting a super star-shaped crumpet.

Children from distant neighbourhoods flooded on to Pip Street, surging into Café Coffee to grab a flyer about the competition, before rushing home excitedly, dreaming of how they would create the prize-winning crumpet. Everyone wanted to win. Everyone wanted to be able to look themselves in the mirror and say "I reinvented the crumpet!" What greater glory could there be? What higher honour?

Of course, Bobby and Imelda wanted to win, too, but mainly they just wanted the competition to be a hit, to boost crumpet sales and keep Bobby on Pip Street. So they practised making their King Crumpet throughout the next few days, until it was perfect. And so, with just three days to go before the grand tasting and winner announcing, they were sitting in Bobby's bedroom, writing out the secret recipe in best, when the doorbell rang. They could hear Bobby's mum laughing downstairs, and then the sound of footsteps coming nearer.

"Look who's here, children," said Bobby's mum, showing in the attractive boy Conkers had seen moving into the house opposite. The boy was tanned, with the wavy blond hair of a film star who loves surfing in his spare time.

"This is Pompey Pasty," said Bobby's mum. "Look, he's brought me some flowers from his garden. How lovely!"

Bobby said hello politely, but Imelda sprang up and began stroking Pompey's arm, beaming up at him.

"I'm Imelda, and this is Bobby, and this is Bobby's room, and we're just writing down our secret recipe for some taste-sensational new crumpets that we're really hoping will win the crumpet competition," she yammered.

"Ahem," coughed Bobby.

"*What?*" said Imelda, flashing a cross look at him. It was the first time she had snapped at Bobby. He didn't like it.

"Secret crumpet recipes?" said Pompey, smiling and sitting down like he owned the place and was Lord of the Entire Street, too, and possibly even Emperor of All Stuff Ever.

Bobby covered the recipe with his hand.

"Don't worry," Pompey said. "I don't much like crumpets *or* cooking. They're just not my thing, you know? Your secret is safe."

"But don't you want to enter the competition?" asked Imelda. "Everyone is talking about it!"

Pompey just shrugged and smiled. Imelda smiled back. Bobby didn't. There was something a bit shark-like about Pompey's eyes. Nice and blue, but a bit dead, too.

The phone rang. It was Great Auntie Mo in Scotland, with details of when she would arrive tomorrow. She was catching the train from Glen Haggis for a visit. Bobby dashed downstairs to ask her for an extra supply of toffees, ready for the crumpets.

Back in Bobby's room, Pompey smiled at Imelda. "You're quite small, aren't you," he said.

"Small by name and small by size," said Imelda, proudly.

"I expect that's really useful for squeezing through little gaps," said Pompey.

"It most certainly *is*," said Imelda, delighted that someone finally understood the positive side of shortness. She was beginning to really like Pompey

Pasty, and so excitedly told him all about the small spaces she had squeezed into and out of in her life.

As she chatted, Pompey's eyes drifted over to the secret recipe. He read the first two ingredients – crumpets, Scottish toffees – and was just about to read on, when Bobby rushed back into the room, snatched up the recipe and stuffed it into his pocket.

The two eyed each other for a moment.

"And anyway, I managed to squeeze free just in time to see an enormous whale swallowing the entire boat," said Imelda, panting.

"Let's go and play on the street," suggested Pompey. "You two can show me round. I want to meet everyone, and I'm pretty sure they would like to meet me, too, wouldn't they?"

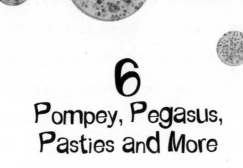

6
Pompey, Pegasus, Pasties and More

Out on the street, Imelda pointed out her home, and number 1, where Jeff the Chalk, the vet nurse, lived. Jeff was a quiet neighbour who never said much. Instead, he chalked out messages on the street, usually about dog poo. He encouraged people to clear up after their mutts, writing things like **DOGS WHO POO DON'T USE THE LOO!**

It was all very hygienic.

Imelda was just showing Pompey the house belonging to the acting family, the Rhubarbs, when Richard Keiths, the oldie from down the road who drove a speedy mobility scooter called Pegasus, raced up the pavement. Mr Keiths was in his seventies, but he didn't let age stop him doing anything. Except perhaps rock climbing. Or being able to stay awake while sitting in a nice comfy chair. But anyway, to prove he had lived fast and *not* died young, Mr Keiths drove his mobility scooter at top speed along the pavements, without a thought for pedestrians.

The children sprang out of Pegasus's way as Mr Keiths screeched to a stop.

"Hey, kiddos, how's it going?" he said.
"It's going brilliantly!" said Imelda, dropping down from the tree she had shimmied up to escape the speeding scooter. "This is Pompey Pasty; he's moved to number 3. Doesn't he look like he should be on telly?"

Mr Keiths rubbed his chin and nodded slowly.

"Any brothers or sisters?" he asked Pompey.

"No, sir," said Pompey. "There was a mix-up at the hospital where I was born.

39

I was nearly swapped with another baby and given to the wrong family. They sorted it out, but it put my mum off having any more children."

"What do your folks do?" asked Mr Keiths.

"They both have jobs in the same office," said Pompey, "doing... Actually, I don't know what they do. Officey stuff, I suppose."

Imelda giggled.

"Oh Pompey, you're so funny," she said, wrinkling up her tiny hamster nose.

"I know," said Pompey, smiling so that his perfect white teeth sparkled in the clear morning light.

"Well, time to split," said Mr Keiths, revving Pegasus. "Need to get to the Co-op for more crisps. I've got a hunger for salt and vinegar."

"It was very nice to meet you, sir," said Pompey.

"Adios, friends," said Mr Keiths, and he sped away.

As soon as Richard Keiths had driven round the corner, the smile drained from Pompey's face and he suddenly looked furious.

"Gah, I'm so *bored*!"

he shouted.

He snapped a branch off a tree and smashed it against a wheelie bin. Bobby and Imelda jumped in shock. Then he picked up some pebbles and lobbed them at Conkers and his little cat friend Coriolanus as they sunned themselves on a wall. The cats ran away to escape the speeding pebbles

(this move is known as a pebble dash).

"Hey!" shouted Bobby. "Leave those cats alone."

Pompey didn't care.

"Come on, Imelda," he said. "Let's go to that café down the road. I've got some money for fizzy drinks."

"Fizzy drinks at Café Coffee?" she said, her eyes lighting up. Imelda wasn't usually allowed fizzy drinks anywhere, let alone in a café.

"Yippee!" she said. "Is Bobby coming, too?"

Pompey looked at Bobby.

"Sorry, I've only got enough for two drinks," he said, walking away and looking completely un-sorry (and also like he had enough for three drinks).

Imelda looked at Bobby, shrugged, and then scampered after Pompey, leaving Bobby alone.

44

7
The Misery List

Bobby watched Pompey and Imelda go to Café Coffee, his fists clenched. In his head, he made a list of reasons to be unhappy about Pompey Pasty's arrival on Pip Street. The List went like this:

1. He seems to have everyone falling at his feet, thinking he's so great. Even Mr Keiths. I don't get it!

2. He tried to read my secret crumpet recipe after saying that he wasn't interested

3. He is stealing Imelda off me. I thought we were best friends. What has got into her?

Bobby went inside, feeling lonelier than a mountaineer who has taken a wrong turn in a snowstorm.

To cheer himself up, he watched his new favourite cartoon, *Mr Positive*. In it, superhero Mr Positive turns baddies good with just the power of positive thinking and looking on the bright side.

Tremendous stuff.

So Bobby tried to do the same. *Cheer up*, he told himself, *at least the secret crumpet recipe is safe.*

Oh no, hang on, actually – *was* it safe?

Bobby rummaged in his pocket, like a squirrel searching for last year's nuts in a haystack. Old tissue – check. Acorn – check. Interesting stone with face of Jesus on it – check.

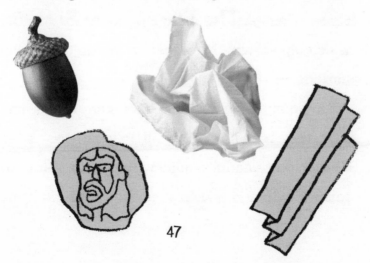

Rummage. Rummage. Rummage. Ah ha! There it was! The recipe! Safe as socks. Phew! Bobby raced up to his room and put the recipe into an envelope. Then he hid it inside his biggest book, **The Big Book of Big Books**, which listed all the hugest books in the world. It included **The Ginormous Book of Words From All Different Languages** and the ancient Chinese legend **The Tale of Twen Shen Bo**, which is absolutely gigantic, but a teensy bit boring.

The recipe was hidden. No one would find it in that book. Least of all Pompey. He didn't seem like much of a reader. So it was safe – or was it? With a jolt, Bobby realized there was one small problem – literally. Imelda! She knew the ingredients of the King Crumpet. Would she blurt the recipe to Pompey? Surely Imelda could keep a secret? Couldn't she?

8
Charming and Alarming

After Bobby had eaten his lunch (it was crumpets –
well, of course it was), he went round to Imelda's
house. He wanted to remind her about MCS level,
but she was out, larking around with Pompey.
Bobby spent a boring afternoon alone, doing
things too boring to mention here – it would ruin
the story – then went to bed with Conkers curled
up on his chest.

The next thing Bobby knew, it was morning. For yes, he had fallen asleep, the night had passed and the cheerful sun had risen on another new day. As it does. And now the competition was just two days away.

Bobby got dressed and went downstairs, yawning like a lion cub, but when he opened the front door to bring the milk in, he almost fell off his feet in surprise. There was a very small Roman lady running past, wearing a toga, with a leafy garland in her curly red hair. Imelda!

"Oh, Bobby," she said, pausing and panting. "I can't stop. Pompey got us tickets to watch that Roman drama, *See You Later, Gladiator*, being filmed. He actually knows the actor who plays Minimus! We're going to have our pictures taken with him, then have an extra big dinner for our lunch, and we might even get to ride in a chariot! It's going to be *absolutely fun*."

"Great," said Bobby, without meaning it.

"Yesterday," Imelda continued, "after fizzy drinks at Café Coffee, Pompey took me to his dad's office and his dad gave us a free calculator, then Pompey stole some sweeties from the Co-op, which was a bit naughty, but super exciting, and then we went to the park and threw twigs at the ducks, which

53

was also a bit naughty, but I don't think the ducks minded. We only hit one, anyway..."

Imelda's long, excited speech ended suddenly as she noticed Pompey coming out of his house dressed as a centurion. Imelda sighed. Bobby could see why. Even though he was beginning to seriously dislike Pompey Pasty, he had to admit he looked good. He just totally rocked the whole skirt and sandals look.

"Hey, Bobby," Pompey said. "I only have two tickets to the show, so unfortunately you can't come. It's a pity. You would have looked great dressed up in something quite plain. Maybe as a slave? Anyway, got to run."

With that, the two raced off, leaving Bobby standing alone. Quite alone. With not a soul for company. Just himself. On his own-some. One. Plus none.

Bobby felt sad. Why was Pompey hogging Imelda like this? She was his friend first and also his crumpet development partner. And why was Imelda falling for Pompey and his silly showing-off ways? All his fizzy drinks and free calculators! Finally, since we're on the subject of whys, why does it feel strange if you brush your teeth with your coat on?

Bobby didn't have the answers, but he did have a headache. Seeing Imelda skipping off with Pompey, worrying about keeping the crumpet recipe at MCS level – it was all stressing his brain. He wanted to grab a stick and smash it against a wheelie bin, like Pompey had the day before. *But hang on*, Bobby thought, coming to his senses. *I would then be just like Pompey. And I am better than him. I am a Cobbler, not a Pasty, and I will never strike a wheelie bin. Never, I tell you!*

This little speech in his head cheered Bobby up, but the cheery feeling didn't last.

For Bobby was about to have

da da duuuuurrrrr
his WORST DAY EVER.

And for this, dear readers, we will need a new
chapter.

9
Bobby's WORST DAY EVER!

Can you imagine what a Worst Day Ever might involve? Fighting a Viking army with only a hot dog for a weapon, then coming home and having to clean the toilet? Learning Spanish for three hours while someone drops cold rice pudding down your vest?

58

Yes, these things are terrible, but Bobby's Worst Day was *worse*. By, like, loads!

It included Bobby stepping on a dog poo (must have been one Jeff the Chalk had missed), Conkers getting stuck up a ladder (cats and ladders are a silly combination), Bobby's mum talking to some

woman for ages on the way to the shops so Bobby had to just *stand* there,

Mr Positive not being on (there was some programme about the price of tractors instead) and nothing to eat but crumpets, with more crumpets on the side, and then crumpets for pudding.

What made it worse – much, much, oh much worse – was that Imelda was probably having her Best Day Ever with Pompey, riding around in chariots, meeting actors and wearing a toga!

WORST. DAY. EVER!!!

Days like this don't fly by, like days full of butterflies and lollipops do. No, they dribble by, like jelly through a sieve.

That's how it was for Bobby. He hung about in his room, nervously checking the crumpet recipe was still safe, then gazing out of the window, thinking lonely thoughts. He waved at Jeff the Chalk, rushing back from the vet's, where he worked. He noticed Mrs Rhubarb driving home from filming the show *Gubbings* (she played an antiques shop owner). He spotted Nathan, playing basketball, wearing his brown dressing gown. Nathan liked to wear his brown dressing gown as much as possible. He loved it like a friend.

Perhaps I should play with Nathan, Bobby thought, when suddenly he noticed Pompey and Imelda coming home. His stomach flipped. Pompey was Squickling Imelda, which is when you squash someone and tickle them at the same time. Bobby felt jealous.

He loved squickling, especially with Imelda.

Bobby banged on the window and waved. Did Pompey glance up? Bobby couldn't be sure. But neither of them waved; they just disappeared into Pompey's house, laughing all the while.

Ha, ha, ha-ritty-ha.

Bobby felt upset, angry and sad – too many emotions all at once! It was uncomfortable; like wearing pants made of miserableness with too-tight elastic. Life is funny, though. Just when you think those pants of pain can't squeeze your bot any tighter, sometimes, if you're lucky, they don't. And that's how it was for Bobby. In all his unhappiness, he had forgotten one thing. Great Auntie Mo was coming to visit! Right now!

Ding dong went the doorbell, and "Helloo, wee man," said Great Auntie Mo, snuggling Bobby into her tartan cape.

It smelled of heather and honey and fresh Scottish air.

Suddenly, Bobby's Worst Day Ever transformed into his Worst Day Ever – But With a Really Good Ending.

"I've brought toffees, too," said Great Auntie Mo. "Lots of them!"

10
Jinty Sporrig Time

Now, remember Great Auntie Mo
is from Scotland, and speaks
with a lovely sing-songy
Scottish accent.
Try reading her words aloud to
help puzzle out what she's saying.
Hoots man and away ye go!

Great Auntie Mo unpacked the toffee boxes from her case and piled them on to the kitchen table.

"And here's some of that Scottish soap your mother likes," she said, unpacking a few boxes of Dougray McFlannel's Highland Hygiene Bars.

"Now donnae get the two mixed up!" laughed Great Auntie Mo, looking at the boxes of brown toffees and the boxes of brown soap. "Soap cleans your feet, while toffee's a treat, you ken?"

Then she and Bobby sat down for a chat, or "a wee jinty sporrig" as she called it, using ancient Scottish words.

Bobby told his great auntie about his exciting new crumpet recipe and how he couldn't wait for competition day.

"Patience, Bobby," said Great Auntie Mo. "You cannae kivver a crumpet."

Then Bobby explained how Pompey seemed to have stolen Imelda from him.

"Och, well, it's always drear when a friend gans astray, but if her heart is true, she'll nay forget you," said Great Auntie Mo, winking.

Bobby wasn't sure about any of this (particularly the bit about kivvering a crumpet – whatever *that* meant) but he was distracted by the sound of Richard Keiths speeding down the pavement on Pegasus and took his great auntie outside to meet him. She offered Mr Keiths a Scottish toffee. He chewed it slowly.

"Good eating, these toffees," he said.

"Right enough," agreed Great Auntie Mo, "but you donnae want tae eat two at once. Doing a double only leads tae trouble."

The pair of oldies had a wee jinty sporrig about the past; the days when Mr Keiths rode a motorbike, not a mobility scooter. Bobby tickled Conkers' ears. And then the afternoon did its daily magic act and *abracadabra!* turned into the evening. Just like that!

"Good talking to you, Great Auntie Mo," said Mr Keiths, revving Pegasus.

"Och, call me Mo, you old fool," clucked Great Auntie Mo, pulling her tartan cape around her.

"So long, Mo," called Mr Keiths. "Stay beautiful."

He sped home.

The sun was slowly setting, like a giant biscuit being dunked into a horizon of tea.

Bobby and his great auntie were just heading indoors when they noticed Mr Pasty parking outside his house. Pompey came to the door.

"Did you get them?" Pompey asked his dad urgently.

"Yes," said Mr Pasty, handing him two giant packs of crumpets, before they both hurried inside.

Bobby stared in shock.

Crumpets?

For the boy who said he didn't like crumpets?

Crumpets?

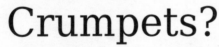

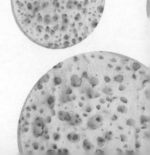

For the boy who didn't like cooking, either? Bobby frowned. It could only mean one thing. Bobby knew it. He sensed it, deep inside his insides. It could only mean this – Pompey was going to enter the competition!

11
Recipe Jeopardy

The next morning, while Pompey Pasty slumbered, occasionally muttering in his sleep "competition, competition, win, win..." Bobby got up. He had slept fitfully. His mind was full of crumpets (not literally, of course) and full of how Pompey must be planning to enter the competition. Bobby was worried. What if Pompey didn't play fair? What if his dislike of cooking meant that, instead of thinking up his own crumpet recipe, he just stole Bobby and Imelda's?

It was a terrifying idea, but not impossible, thought Bobby, who had decided Pompey was untrustworthy and capable of extreme naughtiness.

Bobby went downstairs and found Great Auntie Mo already up. She was sitting in the kitchen singing songs of legendary clansman Flinty McKipper and his passion for porridge as she knitted bedsocks for Richard Keiths.

"Just going to see Imelda," he told Great Auntie Mo, and he sprinted round to her house.

Nathan opened the door, yawning in his brown dressing gown.

"Hello, Bobby," he smiled, sleepily. "Bit early, isn't it?"

"Sorry," Bobby panted. "I need to speak to Imelda."

Bobby vaulted the stairs two at a time, like a gazelle in trainers, then burst into Imelda's room. She was doodling at her desk, but Bobby didn't notice her. Instead, he stood still, staring at the wall by her bed. There were photos of her and Pompey completely covering it: at the TV studios dressed as Romans; drinking fizzy drinks at Café Coffee; squickling; duck-baiting at the park. It made Bobby feel queasy.

"Bobby? Are you OK?" asked Imelda.

Bobby jumped, then looked at Imelda sternly. "I need to talk to you," he said.

"Sure, yes, okey-cokey," said Imelda. She looked guilty; as guilty as a boy scout caught stealing custard creams from a baby.

"Promise me you haven't told Pompey anything about our recipe," said Bobby.

"Course not," she said. "I wouldn't do that."

Imelda's eyes darted to her right.

Bobby knew what that meant. Your eyes go to your left when you're remembering and to your right when you're making something up. Bobby had seen it on a TV programme called *The Facts About Facts*.

Pickled potatoes, Bobby thought, the truth ker-blanging him around the face like a gigantic frying pan – *she's lying!*

His heart sank to his boots, or it would have done if he were wearing boots. Instead, it sank to his trainers.

"Imelda, it's our recipe. We created it," he said. "But I'm worried that Pompey wants to steal it and enter it in the competition. If he does, no one will believe we invented it first. Everyone will

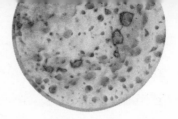

think he did because he's all lovely and charming and la-di-da, and we'll get told off for being stupid copycats. I just know that's what will happen!"

There was a pause. Both children looked worried.

"He has been getting his dad to buy a lot of crumpets lately," Imelda said quietly.

"*I knew it!*" shrieked Bobby. "How much does he know? Have you told him the ingredients?"

"I don't know. No. Nothing," said Imelda, eyes darting to her right again.

"What have you told him, Imelda?" said Bobby. "*Imelda?*"

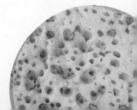

Imelda chewed a lock of her hair like a nervous gerbil.

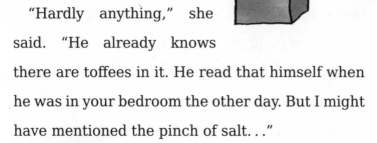

"Hardly anything," she said. "He already knows there are toffees in it. He read that himself when he was in your bedroom the other day. But I might have mentioned the pinch of salt. . ."

"Imelda, NO! That's three out of the six ingredients!" said Bobby.

"I'm sorry," she said, hopping from one foot to the other. "It's just so hard to stand up to him. He keeps chatting about

81

crumpets and the competition, all relaxed like it's no big deal, and going on about how good friends like us should share. Then before you know it you've told him all sorts of vital information." She sighed. "He's just so cool and, you know, I don't want to be rude. . ."

This didn't wash with Bobby.

"Imelda! Come on!" he exploded. "Pompey is tricking you into talking. He knows you're a chatterer. He's trying to get you to blurt all the secret ingredients. Please don't let Pompey ruin our chances, just because you want him to like you."

"What's wrong with wanting to be his friend?" shouted Imelda, suddenly angry.

"He takes me to excellent places which are completely fun and we do one hundred per cent exciting stuff.

For pitta's sake, Bobby, it's better than sitting about in your bedroom reading or whatever!"

Bobby was shocked. He couldn't speak.

Imelda looked a bit shocked, too, realizing she had gone too far. She should have said sorry, right then, but we don't always say the things we should, do we? So instead she muttered, "I have to go. I'm meeting Pompey. He might be cross if I'm late."

And rushed out of the room.

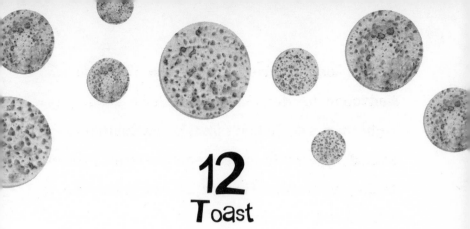

12
Toast

Bobby went downstairs. Nathan was making toast. It felt good to be near Nathan – his brown dressing gown seemed to send out waves of comfort.

"Want some?" Nathan asked Bobby.

"Yes, please," said Bobby, holding out his hand.

Nathan slapped a jammy slice down on Bobby's palm (sticky side up, luckily).

"Problems?" asked Nathan, noticing Bobby's worried face.

"Loads," said Bobby. "Imelda has told Pompey one of the secret ingredients in our crumpet recipe. I'm worried she will tell him the rest."

"Well, on the plus side, she is very proud of that recipe," said Nathan. "She won't even tell me the ingredients, and I'm her brother. But on the minus side, she *is* really into Pompey. In fact, most people on the street seem to love him."

Bobby was chewing this over sadly as he chewed his toast, when suddenly there was a loud, urgent banging at the front door. The boys rushed to open it and found Pompey there, gasping and puffing. They had never seen him so distressed.

"You have to help," he panted. "I took Imelda down to Rabid Pug Wood to tease some weasels, but I lost her! She's lost. In the wood. Rabid Pug Wood. Lost. Oh no..."

He fell to the ground and *almost* cried.

Bobby and Nathan pushed past the almost-crying Pompey and raced down Pip Street towards the woeful woodland.

"We have to find her, Nathan," shouted Bobby, as the two charged along. "That place is dangerous. We have to find her *fast*."

13
If You Go Down To the Wood Today. . .

Bobby ran, as speedily as his trainers-that-were-not-boots would carry him. Nathan followed, his brown dressing gown billowing out behind him like a superhero cape made of towelling.

Neither of them noticed that Pompey was not with them. They were too worried about Imelda. She wasn't scared of much, but she was scared of Rabid Pug Wood. Fair enough, really – it was the spookiest place for miles around, haunted by a dog with a deadly slobbering disease. Nobody wanted to hang out in Rabid Pug Wood.

Not
even
pug-lovers.

Just as the boys were getting close to the wood, a tiny figure rushed out, like a turbo-charged chipmunk. It raced towards Bobby and Nathan, blinded by red curls tangled with leaves and sticks, until *crash!* It collided with Bobby.

"Imelda, it's me!" said Bobby, cuddling his tiny fizzy friend. She shook in his arms, like jelly on a train.

"Oh Bobby, I think I saw it," gasped Imelda. "The rabid pug! At least, I heard it. An awful snuffling noise, spooky enough to frazzle your ears!"

"It's all right. You're safe now," said Bobby. "But why did you go in there?"

"Pompey made me," said Imelda. "He stopped being all friendly about the recipe and starting getting really cross, like he was when he hit that bin. He said if I didn't tell him the other three ingredients, I had to spend fifteen minutes in the wood. I nearly told him, because he *is* cool and all that, but anyway! I wouldn't! I couldn't! I didn't! I remembered about MCS. I remembered what you said in my room. I didn't want to let you down, Bobby."

Bobby hugged Imelda tightly. *She* is *my friend after all*, he thought. *She must be. She chose to face her worst fears, rather than give away the secret recipe.*

"Where is Pompey, anyway?" said Nathan.

The three looked nervously at one another.

"Come on," said Bobby, starting to run. "I've got a bad feeling about this."

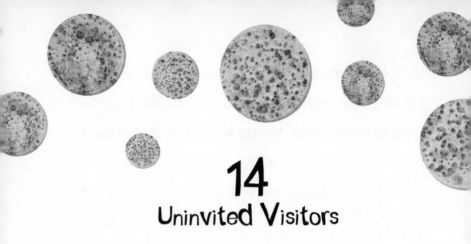

14
Uninvited Visitors

The three children ran back to Pip Street. No sign of Pompey. All quiet. Nathan took Imelda home and Bobby returned to his house. He felt uneasy, but couldn't work out why.

Great Auntie Mo was in the kitchen, still knitting.

"That wee laddie Pompey came tae see you," she said. "Maybe he wants tae make friends? Anyhoo, he's gan up tae yer room."

"*What?*" said Bobby, the blood draining from his freckly cheeks.

"Aye," said Great Auntie Mo, "said he needed to borrow something."

That was why Bobby felt uneasy! Pompey was alone in his room! Bobby rushed upstairs and threw his bedroom door open, making Pompey jump and drop something white. He looked surprised, but not for long.

"Hi, Bobby," he said, like it was completely normal to be in Bobby's room, on his own and uninvited.

"What are you doing?" said Bobby, feeling so angry he thought his eyebrows might explode.

95

"I just wanted to borrow a book," said Pompey, grabbing the first one he could find. It was about origami. This didn't feel right. Pompey didn't seem like a boy who was into folding paper.

"You're searching for the secret crumpet recipe, aren't you?" said Bobby, feeling so angry he thought his hair might catch fire.

"Crumpets!" spat Pompey, looking suddenly cross. "Couldn't care less. What-evs, Bobby!"

"I know you're entering the competition, too," said Bobby, feeling braver than a fireman.

"Maybe I am and maybe I'm not," said Pompey, marching up to Bobby and looking at him in a starey, scary way. "But be sure of one thing. If I do enter your stupid competition, I will win it.

Whatever it takes!"

The two boys stared at each other for a few seconds, and then Pompey flicked Bobby's ear *PLING!* before barging past.

15
Another Fine Mess

Bobby sat down heavily on his bed, rubbing his just-flicked ear. He looked at his room. Pompey had turned it over. Toys were spilled, the duvet was yanked off the bed and books lay in heaps. It looked like a hurricane had ripped through it on its way to pulling the roof off a petrol station and blowing over some pensioners.

Then he noticed the recipe, in its white envelope,

lying on the floor. He snatched it up. It had been opened, just a bit, at the corner. Pompey had found it and begun to open it, but Bobby had burst in just in time! Another thirty seconds and Pompey would have read the recipe.

Bobby sat back down in shock. He didn't even hear Imelda coming in.

"I just wondered if you wanted to play this afternoon," she said, a tiny bit shyly. "I told Pompey I'm busy. After the whole woods thing, I'm not quite sure I can trust him. I never know what he's going to do next."

"Like sneak into my room and find the secret recipe so he can win the competition?" said Bobby.

"Do what-what?" said Imelda.

"Pompey sent me down to the woods to rescue you so he could go through my room," said Bobby, pointing at the devastation.

"The dirty dingbat! Are you sure?" asked Imelda, looking stern, though she was secretly thinking, can anybody with such nice hair be that sneaky?

"Did he find the recipe?" she asked.

"Almost," said Bobby. "But I surprised him before he had time to read it."

"Oh, Bobby. This isn't the end," said Imelda, her eyes as wide as saucers. "You beat him this time, but Pompey won't give up until he gets what he wants."

"Is that so?" said Bobby, his frown beginning to turn upside down. He looked like he was having a bright idea. And that's because he *was* having a bright idea.

"Pompey won't give up until he gets what he wants. So let's give him what he wants," said Bobby, smiling.

"What?" said Imelda. "Have you gone completely doolally?"

"No," said Bobby, grinning. "We will give him the recipe. I never said it had to be the *right* one, did I?"

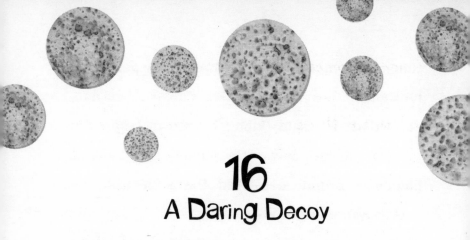

16
A Daring Decoy

Bobby's amazing plan, which he code-named OPERATION CRUMPET CONFUSION, was this:

1. Get a pen
2. Get some paper
3. Write out a decoy recipe, containing fake ingredients, guaranteed to

make a truly horrible crumpet that
could never win the competition
4. Make it easy for Pompey to find

"How do we do number four?" asked Imelda.

"I'm not sure yet," said Bobby, "but I'm working on it."

Just then, Great Auntie Mo popped her head round the door and spotted the untidy state of Bobby's room.

"Och, Bobby," she sighed. "I've ne'er seen such a muckle mess."

"It's not my fault," said Bobby. "Pompey did it."

"Well, Pompey can tidy it up, so he can," she said, tutting. "I'm away to fetch the lad now."

Once Great Auntie Mo had left, Bobby jumped up.

"That's number four on the list taken care of, then," he said, grinning. "We'll leave the fake recipe out on the floor. While Pompey is tidying he won't be able to resist stealing it. But that's fine. That's better than fine, in fact. That's exactly what we want him to do."

17
Tidy-up Time

With no time to lose, Bobby quickly wrote out the trick recipe and put it in an envelope to look just like the original. He even tore the corner. He left it on the floor, amongst the piles of books, and then he and Imelda raced downstairs, just as Great Auntie Mo returned with Pompey.

"Up you go now, you cheeky wee scoundrel,"

she said to Pompey. "A muddlesome room is a cause for gloom – it's time for a tidy."

Pompey slinked upstairs.

Bobby and Imelda sat in the living room watching *Mr Positive* with Great Auntie Mo and Conkers while Pompey cleaned up. Mr Positive had stopped an evil baddie from poisoning a town's water supply by encouraging him to focus on the good things in his life, and sign up for some yoga classes, too. Marvellous stuff.

Finally, they heard Pompey running downstairs. He popped his golden-hairy head around the living-room door.

"All done," he said, grinning slyly. "I'll be off, then."

As soon as they heard the front door slam, Bobby and Imelda rushed upstairs to Bobby's room.

The first thing they noticed was – ooh, how lovely and tidy it looked. Pompey had actually done a smashing job.

Then they looked for the recipe, but it was gone.

"Mission accomplished," said Bobby.

Imelda wasn't so sure.

"What if he guesses it's a fake?" she said.

"Don't worry," said Bobby cheerfully. "Pompey doesn't like cooking. He doesn't even like crumpets. I really don't think he will guess."

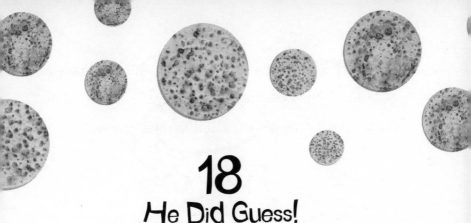

18
He Did Guess!

That's right. He did guess.

But not straight away. Pompey was so certain of success, now that he had the secret recipe, that he didn't rush to try it out. Only late that afternoon did he pop his pinny on and create the crumpet. Then he took a great big mouthful – and immediately spat it all over the kitchen in disgust. BLAH!

Horrible!

"It's a trick," hissed Pompey to himself. "*They tricked me...* But if they think they've beaten me, they are wrong. So wrong. Nobody beats me. I *will* win this competition."

With that, he stormed over to Bobby's house, but Great Auntie Mo had taken Bobby to Pete's Pancake Pit Stop for tea. So he marched round to Imelda's and hammered on the door with his clenched fist. Imelda answered.

"That recipe..." said Pompey, barging in, his blue eyes glinting like wicked sapphires.

Imelda gulped.

"I am only interested in your real recipe, Imelda," said Pompey. "Not in funny little ha-ha fake ones."

"I don't know what you mean," spluttered Imelda, but Pompey knew that she did. And she knew that he knew that she did.

"Bring the true recipe to me by nine p.m.

tonight," Pompey said, jabbing a finger towards Imelda's face, "or I'll find a way to wreck not just your crumpet, but the entire competition tomorrow."

"You wouldn't dare," shouted Imelda, angered by his bullying ways.

"Try me!" said Pompey, and he stormed out.

19
Countdown To Chaos

Imelda waited for Bobby to come home. Seven p.m., no sign. Eight p.m., still no sign. Eight fifteen p.m. You get the idea! As the nine p.m. deadline approached, Imelda became more and more agitated, hopping about at her living room window,

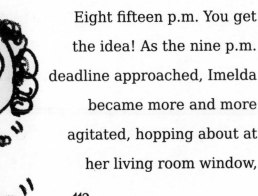

113

staring up and down the street. Finally, at eight thirty p.m., Bobby walked back down Pip Street with his great auntie.

Imelda rushed outside to tell him the terrible news – how Pompey had realized the recipe was fake and vowed to ruin the competition if he didn't receive the real one in the next half hour.

Bobby looked worried, but not panicked. He had a cool head on his shoulders, a belly full of pancakes and absolutely no intention of giving up just yet. In fact, Pompey threatening Imelda made Bobby angry. Angry and determined. He began thinking – hard. Something Great Auntie Mo had said when she first arrived at Bobby's house was rolling around his head. Not the thing about kivvering a crumpet. No, something else. . .

Bobby rushed upstairs and was gone for what seemed like ages to poor nervous Imelda. Finally, at eight fifty-five p.m. exactly, he dashed downstairs. Just five minutes left to save the competition.

Bobby handed Imelda a box of Scottish toffees and the recipe for the King Crumpet.

"Quick," he said. "Take these over to Pompey. Tell him we can't let him ruin the competition, so we give up!"

"No!" shrieked Imelda. "We can't give in to him! There must be another way!"

"It's OK," said Bobby. "There's no more time. And there are more important things than winning. Just go. Hurry!"

Confused and angry, Imelda ran across the road and handed the recipe and the toffees to a very smug-looking Pompey. Then, feeling sad and crushed, like a forgotten raspberry, she went home to bed.

There was nothing more that Bobby could do now. Tomorrow was competition day. The time for crumpet development had passed. All he could do was hope. Hope that justice would be done. Hope that, on the day, the best crumpet would win.

20
Competition Day!

The day of the competition dawned brightly, like a newly polished banjo, and by nine thirty a.m., a crowd had gathered outside the crumpet factory. Amongst them were Richard Keiths on Pegasus, celebrity chef Drew Furry Windowsill and Trevor Scribe from *The Daily Wotsit*, who had brought his camera to report on the thrilling event. The sun shone. The birds sang. There were balloons and bunting and the sound of excited jibber-jabber filling the air. It was like a party outside a crumpet factory.

Hang on,
it *was* a party outside
a crumpet factory!

The competition entrants carefully arranged their crumpety creations on long tables. Here was Nathan's multicoloured crumpet, looking rather brown actually, but at least it matched his dressing

CRUMPET TIME!

gown. Here was Mrs Rhubarb's stellar crumpet, looking a bit like an edible starfish made of dough. Here was Jeff the Chalk's crumpet, long and thin and dusted in sugar, to look like a stick of chalk. Here were iced crumpets and giant crumpets and savoury crumpets; cheesy crumpets and chewy crumpets and chocolate-coated crumpets.

Here, too, was Bobby and Imelda's King Crumpet. They had made a fresh batch early that morning and stood nervously next to their sweet creations. Imelda was wearing a nurse's costume, to calm her jitters. Bobby was looking up and down the line of crumpet competitors. Where was Pompey?

Bobby's thoughts were interrupted by the sight of his dad, standing on a little stage, ready to start the competition.

"Welcome, friends, to what is sure to be a momentous day in the history of tasty snacking!" shouted Mr Cobbler.

The crowd cheered.

"I am delighted to see so many of you here! You will all get to try the crumpets, but I must stress that Mr Furry Windowsill's decision is final."

The crowd clapped and nodded.

"So, without further ado, let us commence the judging!" said Mr Cobbler.

Just then, a figure pushed through the crowd. It was Pompey, carrying a box, which he carefully placed on the last table in the line. Bobby stared as Pompey unpacked his crumpet creations. They looked exactly the same as the King Crumpet.

Once Pompey had arranged his crumpets neatly, he looked over at Bobby. The two boys stared at each other, and then Pompey raised his hand and did an L sign with his forefinger and thumb. *Loser!* Bobby felt his freckly cheeks flush red. He turned away, fuming silently. Bobby was *not* a loser!

The competition was in full swing now, and everyone worked their way along the line of crumpets, tasting and chewing each one. Mr Furry Windowsill tasted Nathan's multicoloured-but-actually-brown crumpet, raised his eyebrows in surprise and made some notes on his clipboard. Then he tasted Jeff the Chalk's chalk-alike crumpet, chewing slowly and thoughtfully as Jeff looked nervously on with his big dark eyes. After further tasting and chewing, the celebrity chef and the crowd reached Bobby and Imelda.

Drew Furry Windowsill bit into the King Crumpet and munched busily. Then he licked his lips, smiled at the two friends, patted Imelda on the head and moved on.

Finally, he reached Pompey.

"This is called Pompey's Toffee Taste Sensation," said Pompey, smiling his film-star smile.

Mr Furry Windowsill smiled back. Everyone tucked in. Bobby and Imelda watched nervously.

The crowd seemed to be enjoying Pompey's creations. Everyone was smiling and nodding to one another. Drew Furry Windowsill did a happy thumbs up. Pompey grinned. Bobby felt anxious. Imelda felt sick.

Then something wonderful happened: something bizarre; something peculiar; something bonkers! From the corners of the munching mouths, bubbles appeared. Tiny at first, like washing-up foam.

Then bigger and bubblier. The more the people chewed, the more the bubbles came, tumbling from their mouths in sticky, frothy clouds.

Everyone began to stare and point.

They opened their mouths in alarm, letting cascades of toffee bubbles splosh down their chins.

They tried to speak, but the foamy toffee mess got in the way.

"Mot's mappening moo uth?" they said, frothing up like a hair wash with extra shampoo.

"Yes, what *is* happening to them?" said Imelda, looking at Bobby, who was grinning his biggest grin.

"Mot mav moo mun?" shouted celebrity chef Drew Furry Windowsill. "Bis bere boap in da mumpets?"

"Boap? Boap?" cried the crowd, their clotted-up mouths mangling their Ss.

Pompey looked confused and cross. He didn't understand, but he guessed he was in trouble. Trevor Scribe's camera flashed as the people turned on the crumpet mucker-upper. Pompey began to back away, but Mr Keiths headed him off on Pegasus, asking him to explain himself.

"I just wanted to make a tasty toffee crumpet," said Pompey.

"You just wanted to steal our recipe for a toffee crumpet, you mean," said Bobby, pushing through the crowd.

Everyone turned to hear Bobby speak.

"Pompey couldn't make up his own crumpet, so he bullied and threatened Imelda until she handed over our recipe and the special ingredient, Scottish toffees," explained Bobby. "Little did he know I had swapped some of those toffees for soap."

"Bo!" said the crowd, still bubbling.

"I cut up some Scottish soap that looks just

like toffees into sweet shapes," explained Bobby. "Then I wrapped these soapy fakes up in shiny papers. I wasn't sure it would work, but it did. Pompey was fooled!"

SOAP

Dougray McFlannel's Highland Hygiene Bars

Och Aye! Highland Toffee

From here   to here

to him

The people gasped and
gurgled some more.
"I'm sorry you
all had to suffer,"
added Bobby,
looking at the
frothing crowd,
"but now you
can see that he is a
cheating little cheater!"

It was true. The crowd no longer thought of
Pompey as charming. Finally, they could see through
him and his scheming ways, like a superhero with
X-ray vision can see through your trousers and find
out what colour pants you're wearing.

"Did you cheat, Pompey?" asked Mr Furry Windowsill, finally able to speak after rinsing his mouth with a litre of water. "That's an instant disqualification, I'm afraid."

"So what if I took their recipe!" shouted Pompey, his blue eyes glinting angrily. "That boy and this mini menace don't deserve to win. I do! Don't you see? I'm better than all of you and your silly little crumpets put together. Better looking, more cunning, more cool, just MORE! And another thing..."

But Pompey didn't get the chance to finish his sentence. Imelda reached into her pocket, found two of Great Auntie Mo's Scottish toffees, ran up to Pompey and popped both into his mouth.

Pompey bit down on the toffees – and immediately regretted it. This was too much chew. His jaw ached, his mouth filled with thick toffee, his teeth tingled. He was "doing a double", and it had, as Great Auntie Mo warned, led to trouble.

Speechless, chewing and dribbling, Pompey was led away by his father. The crowd watched in silence as the boy, with a mouth full of toffee and a face red with shame, slinked home.

21
Victory!

With Pompey gone, Bobby felt a great surge of joy. He had done it. His crazy soap-sudded toffees had bubbled all over Pompey's attempt to win the competition. Fair play had won the day. The King Crumpet was safe. Imelda was by his side. And Pompey had had his just deserts – crumpet style!

"Well done Bobby and Imelda," said Drew Furry Windowsill. "We can't have foul play in this competition. You've rooted out the wrongdoer, and by thrilling means, too. I'm sure I speak for everyone here when I say, well done. And don't worry about us all eating soap – after all, it's not often you have a mouthwash and a crumpet at the same time, is it?"

The crowd laughed in a sticky sort of way.

"Now, I think it's about time I started the final judging," said Mr Furry Windowsill.

The chef examined his clipboard and chatted quietly to Mr Cobbler, taking one last look at all the crumpets.

"And the winner is. . ." he said, before pausing

for dramatic effect. "Mr E Dam from Dip Street for his Cheesy Dutch Crumpet. Simple, tasty, delicious."

The crowd roared and clapped, but Imelda and Bobby looked at each other in shock. The King

Crumpet had not won and they were disappointed. Until, that is, Bobby remembered something vital.

"It doesn't matter who wins," he said to Imelda, smiling suddenly. "With people this excited about crumpets, Dad's factory will be busy again and we won't have to move!"

"You're right," agreed Imelda, brightening instantly. "This is all great! You can stay and we are best friends and everything's good. It's just all pure good."

They hugged, until Mr Furry Windowsill tapped them on their shoulders and draped two medals around their necks.

"For services to truth and fair play," he said, "and for making a very fine caramel crumpet, too.

It was close, but the Dutch cheese just tickled my savoury taste buds."

The crowd cheered again and the two children beamed with pride. It was a proud moment. A moment to be proud of. A moment in which to feel genuine pride.

And so, holding hands with Imelda and Great Auntie Mo, Bobby walked back to Pip Street, with Richard Keiths driving Pegasus alongside, dabbing at his mouth as the last bubbles popped up.

"All this toffee tomfoolery has done me in," he said. "No offence, Mo, but I think I'll stick to salty crisps from now on."

"Och, no bother," she said, smiling. "Better for your teeth, anyway!"

"What's left of them!" said Mr Keiths, chuckling. Then everyone laughed, and goodness, it felt marvellous.

22
Everyone Loves
a Cheesy Crumpet

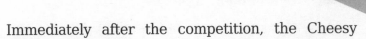

Immediately after the competition, the Cheesy

Dutch Crumpets went into production and became hits with snack-lovers throughout the land. Mr E Dam got his name on the packet and was happy, but so was Bobby.

141

Sales of the Cheesy Dutch Crumpets were massive. Mr Cobbler kept his job and even got a pay rise. The Cobblers would be staying on Pip Street. To celebrate, Bobby and Imelda knocked up a giant batch of King Crumpets. Although their recipe had not won the competition, it was still a hit with their friends and neighbours.

But what about Bobby's narky neighbour Pompey? What became of him? You'll never guess. No, seriously, you *will* never guess, so I'll tell you. . .

The day after the competition, a sports car pulled up on Pip Street, driven by a handsome, golden-haired man in a very expensive suit. He knocked at Pompey's door. Pompey answered. The two blondies looked at each other. The resemblance was striking. They were like two peas in a pod. Two knees on a bod. Two fleas on a cod. Basically, they looked *really* similar.

"Dad?" said Pompey.

"Son," said the man, who can only be described as Pompey's real dad. His name was Sebastian Century.

"So that mix-up in the hospital really *did* happen," said Pompey. "I knew it! I always felt I was more than just a Pasty."

"I read all about your crumpet craziness in *The Daily Wotsit*," said Sebastian Century. "I said to myself, this guy looks like my son and acts like my son. I must find him so he can help run my multinational business. And so here I am. Now let's get you out of this dreary little place."

With that, Pompey jumped into his new dad's very fast car and the double Centurys sped away.

That was the last time Pompey set foot on Pip Street. It was no loss. In fact, it was a gain, in the form of chubby, dark-haired Dave, Paddy and Patricia's real son, who left the Centurys' home and came to live opposite Bobby. Dave was nice. Dave was normal. Dave didn't randomly attack wheelie bins with sticks or steal secret recipes.

Better still, he wanted to be friends with Bobby, Imelda and Nathan. And being jolly nice chaps, they wanted to be friends with him, too.

At last, order had returned. Pip Street was peaceful again. For good? We can only hope so. But we cannot be sure. No one can predict the future – not even weathermen. No one can guess what's round the corner. No one can see into tomorrow. What is tomorrow, anyway? What is time? What is space? What is anything? What is the end? Is this it? Is this the end? Yes, my friends,

it is,

for now. . .

BOBBY'S BURNING QUESTIONS

As we saw in Chapter 1, Bobby enjoys thinking and pondering. And he's always asking questions. Here are some that have popped into his head recently. . .

- Is an ant smarter than a baby?

- Is there a part of our body that we can't move?

- If diamonds are so hard, what happens when you shoot one?

- What's worse: teenagers or tourists?

- What noise does an iguana make?

We don't have the answers to thse juicy ponderings, but that's OK. Sometimes it's just good to wonder.

ANAGRAMS

(CLUE: THINGS YOU CAN EAT AND PEOPLE ON THE STREET)

1. Cut Perm

2. Meaty Pop Spy

3. Heating Held Off

4. Mr Made

5. Dinky Frizz

6. Again Emu Otter

Answers: 1. Crumpet, 2. Pompey Pasty, 3. Highland Toffee, 4. Mr E Dam, 5. Fizzy drink 6. Great Auntie Mo

CREATE YOUR OWN CRACKING CRUMPET

YOU TOO CAN INVENT YOUR VERY OWN CRUMPET. SIMPLY START WITH A PLAIN ONE AND BUILD FROM THERE.

Here is a list of tip-top toppings to kick start your crumpet creativity. . .

- Jam, squirty cream and sprinkles

- Butter, honey and a squeeze of lemon

- Chocolate spread and flaked almonds

- Peanut butter and banana

- Pizza topping — tomato sauce, mozzarella, basil

- Rocky Road topping — mini marshmallows, nuts, chocolate chips

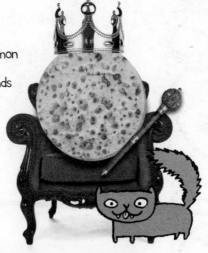

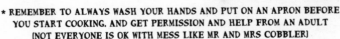

* REMEMBER TO ALWAYS WASH YOUR HANDS AND PUT ON AN APRON BEFORE YOU START COOKING. AND GET PERMISSION AND HELP FROM AN ADULT (NOT EVERYONE IS OK WITH MESS LIKE MR AND MRS COBBLER)

LOOK OUT FOR MORE

ADVENTURES

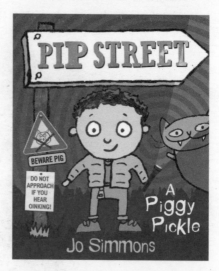

COMING SOON!

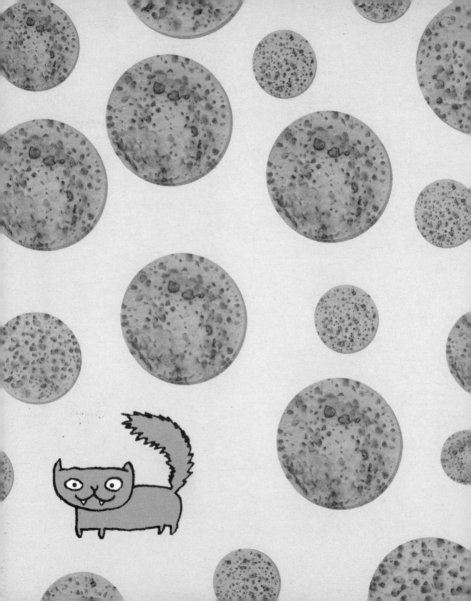